The Horse Trader

Om KIDZ
An imprint of Om Books International

King Krishna Deva Raya was very fond of horses. He never spared money when it came to buying well-bred horses. He was known for owning some of the country's best horses.

One day a horse trader from an Arabian country came to his court and announced, "I have some fine horses for sale. They are the best Arabian steeds in the whole world. I have brought a horse to show you. If you like it, I can send for the others."

The King was very excited by the offer, as the only breed he didn't have in his stables were Arabian steeds.

He saw the majestic horse standing outside his palace and immediately offered to buy the whole lot of them. The man took an advance of 5000 gold coins. He promised to return with the whole set of horses in two days and went away.

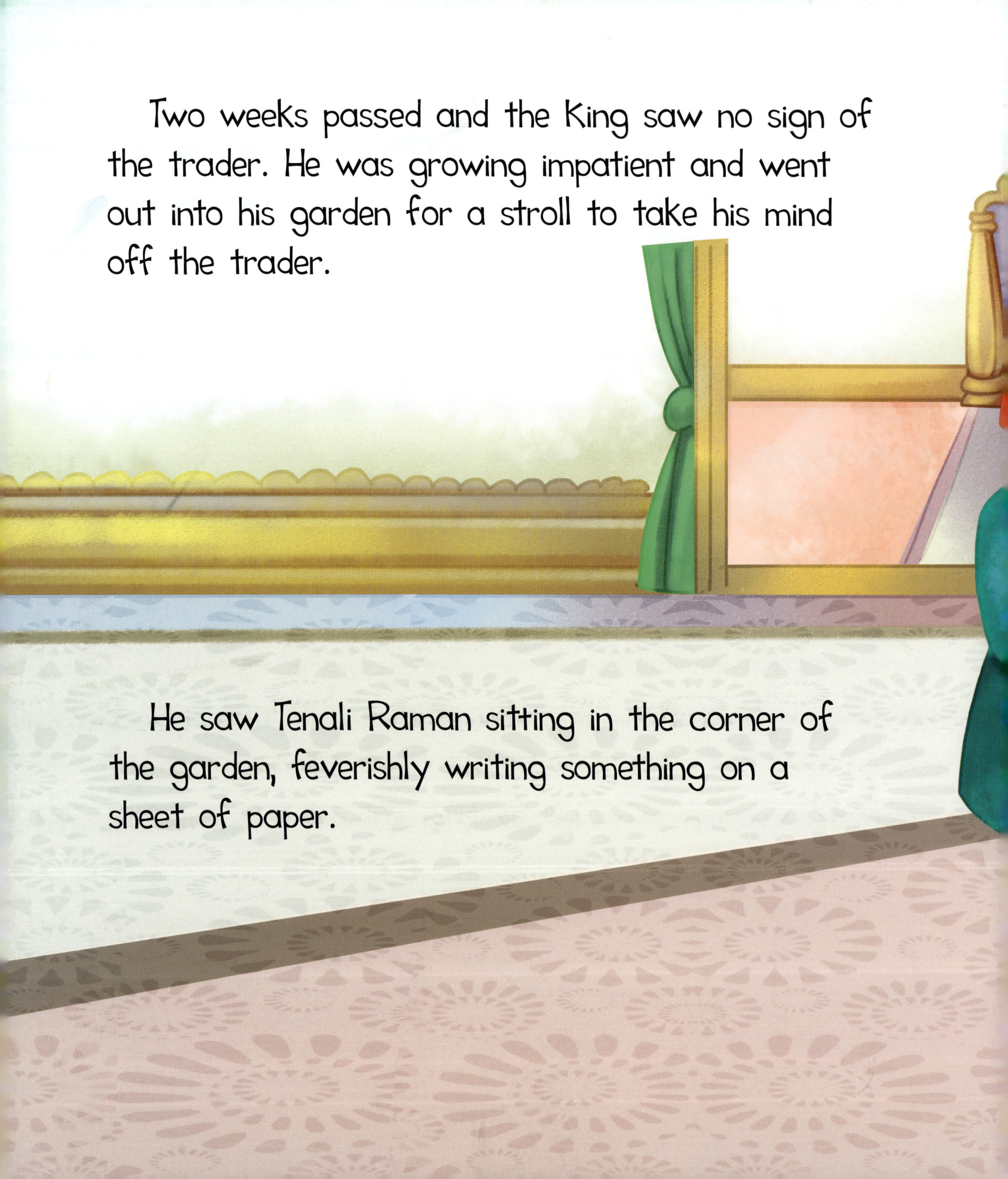

Two weeks passed and the King saw no sign of the trader. He was growing impatient and went out into his garden for a stroll to take his mind off the trader.

He saw Tenali Raman sitting in the corner of the garden, feverishly writing something on a sheet of paper.

"What are you writing, Raman?" he asked. Raman continued to write without looking up. The King was very curious and demanded, "I command that you show me what you are writing, immediately."

"Well, you may not like it, but I'm making a list of the greatest fools in the kingdom," said Raman.

The king was astonished at the reply. "Hand over the paper to me," he said. "I need to see the names in there. I am sure that the list you have written must be quite sensible and true."

Raman handed over the paper and within a moment he heard the King's voice thundering, "How dare you write my name on top of the list Raman?

Isn't this an insult to your King? I demand an explanation. You think I am a fool!"

"Any man who would give 5000 gold coins to a complete stranger and expect him to return, is a fool!" replied Raman.

"Oh! So that's what is troubling you," said the king."You think the man won't return. What if he does? You will be wrong then."

"In that case," said Raman with a twinkle in his eye, "I'll scratch out your name and put his there." The King understood the wise words behind Raman's wit and never made any major decisions without consulting his beloved courtier.